A Visit To GRANDMA'S

Nancy Carlson

PUFFIN BOOKS

PUFFIN BOOKS
Published by the Penguin Group
Penguin Books USA Inc., 375 Hudson Street, New York, New York 10014, U.S.A.
Penguin Books Ltd, 27 Wrights Lane, London W8 5TZ, England
Penguin Books Australia Ltd, Ringwood, Victoria, Australia
Penguin Books Canada Ltd, 10 Alcorn Avenue, Toronto, Ontario, Canada M4V 3B2
Penguin Books (N.Z.) Ltd, 182–190 Wairau Road, Auckland 10, New Zealand

Penguin Books Ltd, Registered Offices: Harmondsworth, Middlesex, England

First published in the United States of America by Viking Penguin,
a division of Penguin Books USA Inc., 1991
Published in Puffin Books, 1993

1 3 5 7 9 10 8 6 4 2

LIBRARY OF CONGRESS CATALOGING-IN-PUBLICATION DATA
Carlson, Nancy L.
A visit to Grandma's / Nancy Carlson   p.   cm.
"First published in the United States of America by Viking Penguin . . . 1991" — T.p. verso.
Summary: When Tina and her parents go to spend Thanksgiving with Grandma
in her new Florida condominium, they are surprised to find that she
is very different from when she lived on the farm.
ISBN 0-14-054243-4
[1. Grandmothers—Fiction. 2. Beavers—Fiction.
3. Thanksgiving Day—Fiction. 4. Florida—Fiction.]
I. Title
[PZ7.C21665Vi   1993]   [E]—dc20   93-18607   CIP   AC

Printed in the United States of America
Set in 16-point Weidman

Florida

S

• Pensacola

• Tallahassee

• Jacksonville

• Orlando "FUN"

TAMPA

St. Petersburg

Pompano
Fort Lauderdale
• Miami

Everglades

**Dedicated to
Grandpa John
who <u>loved</u>
warm weather**

Happy Mother's Day
Mary Lou!

Love,
Becky, Jim
Graham &
Rachel

Tina and her parents were going to fly to Florida to
visit her grandmother in her new home for Thanksgiving.

"I'll sure miss the old farm," said Dad,
"but I can't wait to see Grandma."

"Ahh—I can almost smell Grandma's pumpkin pies," said Dad.
"I can almost taste her turkey and stuffing," said Tina.

Tina, Mom, and Dad couldn't believe
their eyes when they saw Grandma.

"Is that you, Grandma?" asked Tina.
"Are you okay?" said Dad.

"I feel great!
Hop in!!!" said Grandma.

When they got to Grandma's condo,
it wasn't at all like the old farm.

"Well, I suppose you'll start baking pies now!" said Dad.
"No time! I'll pick some up at the store
after aerobics," said Grandma.

"Store-bought pies! Grandma has always
baked her own pies," complained Dad.

After her aerobics class, Grandma invited her
friends Bill, Dottie, Vernice, and Dorothy over.

They played charades until midnight!

On Thanksgiving morning, Grandma got up to go to tap-dance class.
"Aren't we having your famous cinnamon rolls?" said Mom.
"Goodness' sakes, no! That's not good for you. There are health shakes
  in the fridge," said Grandma.

"Grandma has changed," said Mom.
"I hope she's home in time to make
turkey dinner," said Tina.

When Grandma got home, she told them they were
meeting friends at Monti's Fish and Chips.

"What, no turkey dinner? I want Thanksgiving
like it always was," said Tina.

But Monti's was great!

Tina discovered she loved stone crab.

All during dinner, Bill pulled quarters out of
Tina's ears. Vernice told funny stories,

and Dottie had a purse full of candy.

After dinner, they all went to the condo for pie.
"I must say, this pie isn't as good as mine," said Grandma.

"I like it better,"
Dad whispered to Tina.

"Remember at the farm we used to take a
sleigh ride after dinner?" said Tina.

"Well, we can't take a sleigh, but we can
take a ride! Let's go!" said Grandma.

"This is fun!" said Tina.

When it was time to go home, Tina, Mom, and
Dad agreed it had been a great Thanksgiving.
"We'll be back in the spring," said Mom.

"Be sure to make reservations at Monti's!" said Tina.
"And don't forget to buy those good pies!" said Dad.